MY HALF VERSION

ASK YOURSELF OVER CUP OF COFFEE AND DISCOVER YOUR ANOTHER HALF

SHUBHAM TOMAR

ISBN 979-888569401-8

Contents

Introduction

Firstly, I want to thank you for choosing this book as part of your library for this year.

You know self-retrospection is one of the great exercise one can do for their development in their lives. It could be related to their professional or personal life. And asking a few questions to yourself can gives you the glimpse of the better version of yourself. By asking and revealing the thoughts hidden inside your subconscious mind can unveils the another you. I pen down the examples and thoughts to let the world ponder on themselves launching the capabilities installed inside them.

We spend time with family, friends and even with our beloved gadgets all day. I want you to stop a little and spend some time with yourself. Who knows, you would end up finding a new friend of yourself.

I hope this book would bring a clarity to yourself and many truths which were there already waiting for you to be get introduced. Make sure you are comfortable for accepting and ready to have a conversation with a friend before you deep dive into this book. Also, it would be great if you make notes out of it to work in future if needed.

Knowing self with positive mind frame can makes your introduction to the pinnacle of success you desire and accomplish all objectives in your to do list.

I wish you good luck for the journey with this book.

Again, Thanks a lot from the bottom of my heart.

I wish you great learnings ahead.

Stay Healthy

1

Overcoming Problems

"We cannot solve our problems with the same thinking we used when we created them." - By Albert Einstein

We all have problems in our lives. It could be professional, financial, family etc from different sources and reasons. Having problems in life is nothing new or we can summarise problems as a part of life. The way we try to tackle that depends on the mindset and great wisdom. Some would find to pass an examination a challenge while some pass same, like an expert. But here passing an exam is not only a thing if we see every challenge in life as an exam and consider its solution as result. You might be expecting to get that result as Pass. It is not a matter of how much time you have devoted to that problem, here question arises how much effective effort you have made to reach your goal. In professional life some folks get promoted to higher position at very early stage of life while many find it hard to get same.

Don't lose hopes, rather ask yourself when you have results,

Are You Satisfied with results?

Have you given your cent percent?

Is this the same results what you expected?

If all these comes with an answer YES.

Congratulations, it implies, you did it. It's time for cherish and reward yourself.

Here comes a big BUT if any of these above question gives you NO. Why? what goes wrong? what made it a different answer as per your expectations. Hey, don't get disheartened with the results. It's not time to sorrow on results or your life. It is not a time to waste upon finding a shoulder to cry upon or sympathise yourself by saying it's not my cup of tea. If you did anything alike, you have made another blunder of life. You are disrespecting your talent, your time, your potential and majorly YOURSELF.

Rather Its time to go back, Analyse the problem once again

and ask

What made your answer as NO?

Where you lacked in making efforts?

Try to find these Answers and ask again

Are you ready to give one more shot?

If above question comes with again NO. Why NO? It should be YES always if you really wanted to be live your life without any regrets because warriors never regret. They fight till they get what they wanted, till they die in battleground. Are you Dead? Definitely not, as corpse never read. Cadaver don't think, don't plan their life, and try to solve problems preferably they REST IN PEACE. I don't think we are among them. We do talk, breathe, walk, and analyse. Even we are better than ZOOMBIES.

Now here comes the part of answer YES, I am ready to play another shot for life. Your failures definitely gives the KEY to Success that needs to be found out.

What made your answer NO to expected outcomes?

What was the break point?

Pick that one and I am pretty sure if you got that correct answer you are going to accomplish your goal. Pull your arrow backward and get ready to hit the aim you have decided. It's your arrow so you are the only one going to decide the factors at which moment and fraction of second you need to free it considering air directions and speed. If you don't get a weak point, you must be ready to repeat the whole cycle.

The problems use to come like a storm in one's life. Everyone has their own approach to tackle them. Some use the traditional known methods while some define their newly built approach. It inevitable that problem would come. The only thing which matters is how you look towards that. It's you only who have to manage yourself to overcome with it. After it comes to an end you won't realise how disastrous it was, but what lefts behind is your new personality.

Sometimes it happens in life, I am pretty sure that you have also faced this kind of situation where you have had a perception about problem that it's critical to solve, but when you even had taken a first step towards its resolution it got solved. So, we shouldn't be creating any beliefs until we analysed it. It's worst idea to let problem be aside as it seems to be inflexible without putting a thought of resolving it. Let me take this opportunity to remind you that it was a problem to have a communication over letter till last century which leads to the conversion of great invention of century and brought a revolution in technology with devices called mobiles and computers.

There are no rules of running away of problems and no age limits of having them either. Everybody is prone to this word, and they must come over with it by themselves. Though you can get hints from your surroundings to resolve, but ultimately what matters is you.

How Problem looks like?

How difficult it is?

Have you faced it earlier?

Do you know any who had similar experience?

You need to analyse it with these sets of question. It's not mandatory to answer only these questions but you should be preparing a lot of questions as much you can. After answering every question from your set, you need to connect the dots for your solution. You will find the key to unlock the quest within your answers, if not then prepare more questions related to it.

The great algorithm *Divide and Conquer* can plays significant roles for overcoming any problem. The problems need to be understood so that we can overcome with that by breaking it into chunks so we can tackle each slice of it with great compassion. You can master yourself in dealing the problems with this approach giving back a tough fight to any complication.

2
Setting Goals

*"Goals are not only absolutely necessary to motivate us.
They are essential to really keep us alive."*
By Robery H. Schuller

Many people talk about what they are going to do but how many already decided and started working on it. Life is only 10 percent of what happened to you and rest is all what you have done in respond to that. Goal is what your expectations are and how much desperate you are towards it would be deciding the pace of your life. Success of your goals can't be decided by anybody in this universe except you. You are the exception to decide the path, pace, and ultimate destination where you wanted to be. No one can help to make plans or roadmap your destiny except your hardship and commitment towards your goal.

Here comes the great saying

"The wolf on top of the hill is not as hungry as wolves still climbing the hill"

It defines how much hungry you are to achieve you goal. You need to be hungry and keep going without thinking of having rest. We are very well aware of famous story of *"Rabbit and Turtle Race"* in which The Turtle Won the race with continuous efforts and dedication keeping goal in head, which concludes *"Slow and Steady Wins the Race"* but in my opinion clear picture of goal should be there in your head.

What have you wanted?

How can you achieve the goal?

What can be done to get your goal?

Are you on track?

You need to ask yourself, millions of times, above questions that could be helpful in deciding the goal. Your goal could be getting a promotion, getting good grades, getting good pay or it could be anything that's going to make you better from what you are at present. Nobody in this world would be affected at what time you get up from bed. Nobody cares about how hard you are working towards your goal. You need to become better version of yours.

Are you getting better every day?

Are you having something new today?

Did you get your version updated today as well?

Ask these questions every single day before going to bed. No one is going to come and ask about your enhancement. It doesn't make sense to any rather it does to you only.

It's you who is going to decide what and how you are going to make a difference to become better version. It's you who is going to decide whether you are going to party tonight, read a book, going to attend some trainings, or going to spend time in gym. Nothing what you do in life is good or bad, but your present action decides your future indeed. It depends on you only what you consider distractions for your life or goal and how you are going to tackle them. Make sure you are running in race and need to complete that goal. If somehow you get injured, get up, make sure you walk, if you can't walk crawl but don't stop. Being stopped is not a solution to any problem that you have. You need to be focused to your goal.

You need to get in love with you, your goal and your life. You need to work to get better version of yours, seek better direction in your life. Might you need to sacrifice today for something to see a better version of you, don't get discouraged and demoralised your heart and mind. That could be disastrous for being better. As in journey of being better and accomplishment of your goals your Mind and heart were only two friends who are going to support you. Mind will give you aid as wisdom of choosing the right directions while having coordination with your heart a sense of relief and happiness of being going forward on your path. So, you also need to support them while making tough decisions of sacrificing.

What is next version of you?

What would be next update you wanted to have?

What changes are needed?

Ask above questions again and again.

"It is not the strongest of the species that survive,

nor the most intelligent,

but the one most responsive to change" By Charles Darwin

Are you done with your evaluation?

If not, Plan it!!!

3
Focused

"The time that leads to mastery is dependent on the intensity of our focus." - By Robert Greene

Today is having all great potential opportunity and power to make changes. Don't think twice to do something that can make achievement in your skills. It's a time to make correction for yesterday and future better. Today is what you need to build so your future TODAY would be at better than present TODAY.

If you want something in life, want to achieve or acquire something, want to change something in your life is not easy as some people make us feel. Living a dream, overcoming your challenges and your negative points is quite hard. Point to be noticed is that it's hard not impossible or unattainable.

To acquire your empire of success you should be knowing what your ultimate destination is.

"Whenever you want to achieve something.

All the universe conspires in helping you to achieve that goal"

- By Paulo Coelho

If we want to get a job in dream company or someone wants to be an entrepreneur with millions of profits in bank account is achievable. Yes, you read it correctly and many folks would agree with my statement because might they have already got this, but what about those whose are still having hurdles to reach this place would deny. Some would say "Everyone is not same in terms of knowledge or resourcefulness", I agree with them, but my question arises for them is that "Those who have great empires, who owns lavish account statements were always had this?" My answer would be big NO. No matters who you are, your everyday can't be the same. Whether you are rich living in Silicon Valley or poor in some slum. You will for sure would be having bad days which can leads to lose the focus of your goal. But those who remained intact were the clincher of the race leading their failures way back. You must touch the finish line after which you can smile at the failures saying them *"Better luck next time"*. The sense which you would be getting after this smile is inarticulate by anyone in this entire universe.

Everyone in this world wants to be rich without an exception. Different people see abundance differently in their lives. Some of us need abundance of happiness, some would say peace or majority expected answer would be money. If I would ask them

"How much you think would be enough for them?"

The answer is for sure would be diverse and won't have consistency to that. Another question again would be asked

"What were you doing for having that plentifulness to achieve?"

We can expect contrast with the answers as well. Some of the examples of answers as follows

- They are working hard
- They were loyal to their job
- They were learning new skills to earn more
- They were doing overtime
- They were doing freelance work as well apart from job to earn some passive income

Now here come the part to ask yourself

Whether you can achieve your goal with approach you were following?

Are you in middle of your success?

Are you delighted with your progress?

If your answers give you uncertainty for your goal to achieve, my dear you need to do some homework and plan it with proper vision and focus your target that you want to accomplish in life. We all have fixed twenty-four hours in a day and sixty minutes in an hour. Each any every action you commit every second of your day reflects in your achievements. Usain Bolt "The Fastest Man" till date have not achieved this title or record overnight. For running

100m with full strength and velocity is the resultant of Hours and Years outcome. So, if you think of getting lottery and accomplish your desires in wink of an eye, I will say you were having wrong notion of having success in your wallet. You need continuous focus and hard work without any deviations to achieve it.

If you were working on any project or wanted to have something in life, you must have roadmap to go. Without which you were unable to decide which path is correct to reach your ultimate destination. You need to plan each and every single step you take towards it. Your mind should have clear picture of what and how your success looks like. If you are having clarity with the thoughts makes it easiness for achieving.

For any goal one should be prepared with prototype for having easy execution of your ideas. You need to focus of every step so you can plan it and prepare yourself for any upcoming hurdles on your way. One should keep in mind that problems do come when you walk any path. It depends on how much you were prepared for it already in advance with clear visions. The more you would focus on the goal more you would be able to discover the complications on your path, and you would be able to conquer them easily if you had identified it well in your planning process.

Trust me going through these ups and downs in life you will find more exhilaration than roller coaster rides. Defeating your problems with proper approach and planning gives a different kind of thrill. You would be able to do so only if you were focused and able to identify all problems and hurdles coming.

Let me take you through an example so you would be able to get why being focused is more important in getting success. One of my friend Aarav, who was having a job, earning good money. At the day end was not happy with rigid job profile. He used to go to gym where he had collaborated with lots of people and cherish the time spent over there. Once he pondered on his life and started thinking

What he wants to achieve in life?

How it can be achieved?

What were the challenges to come?

After that he got some clues, or we can say he got a clear goal he wanted. He resigned from his job. He went for fitness coach certification and excelled that. He became the fitness coach to very known personalities in world. And you won't believe he is earning a lot more than what he got in his previous job.

So, I hope you would get some clear thoughts of what being focused mean, it doesn't mean to do work continuously in some direction but also you need to analyse the path you were on and problems in between. Many would question that he was lucky because its not easy to quit and follow other thing. If this question came across to your mind as well let me first say I agree with your beliefs, but you didn't realise it's not easy to get success. Again, let me take back to story to throw some more light that he didn't got these well-known personalities as client on his door steps. He worked hard to get contacts and building up image to show his skills in front of this world where you need to create opportunity for yourself no one please mind that no one would come to give success as donation.

4

Confidence

"Your success will be determined by your own confidence and fortitude"

By Michelle Obama

When you took up any project or lead any firm you should have confidence, and that confidence is not expected from others but your inner selves. The first person that shows confidence in you is none other than yourselves. The higher trust you show to self the virtue of confidence rises. The confidence not only brings up the leadership in you but also make you life easier to tackle the situations in life.

It's not only belief but great leaders also mentioned about being confident what you do. One's life becomes how and what he thinks of. If someone thinks that he can't do a particular task, no matters of any force present in world can make it possible to change the perception. By just changing the belief and having a confidence for accomplishing a task, symbolise that you are already started.

We can take any example from history or present that can show us the power of confidence. Confidence in my view is powerful tool that one can have. Let me mention the name of Jose Salvador Alvarenga who got lost in sea. It's the tool that made it possible for his survival in sea is the confidence making him record holder of longest solo survivor with 438 days in his account.

We face ups and downs in our life. We encounter failures as well on the road of success. Confidence is the one of the vital tools which plays a critical role for boosting us towards achievement of goal. It plays role like a turbo speed booster to car that is essential to win the race. You need to inculcate it with continuous efforts and preparation.

We can have different emotions like fear, doubts, worries which can pull our legs making journey difficult reaching the goal but having confidence can play one man army role. Once you lose it no one can save you losing the war. One of the examples which comes to my mind while realising the importance of confidence is Tug of War game played in famous series "*Squid Game*" which rightly displayed the need showing weaker team got won with having high confidence in themselves.

While you take any task in your account you should ask yourself

Whether you can do this task?

Are you capable of doing it?

Do you have enough knowledge for it?

If any to all above questions marked Yes, then we can proceed to our task. If any or all of them replicate with answer as No, you need to work on it until it turns out to be Yes.

Many of us lose the confidence when we got surrounded or work with highly qualified and experienced folks. It's human nature that we don't want ourselves to get discourage, but we only need high confidence in ourselves for surviving in any circumstance. Believe me it gives a immense pleasure to gain knowledge and get way ahead of your mates absorbing all experience in little period. It's not necessary to lead a team of high experienced folks if you possess little experience compared. We have tons of names like Sundar Pichai, Satya Nadella who were among great CEOs of multinationals firms and under them many highly experienced worked. It's just matter of confidence that company showed in them to lead.

Confidence is powerful tool that is part of everyone life whether being a student, president of country or solider. Not only it's required for working on some tasks or accomplish a goal but in relationships as well. We need to have a confidence on ourselves first. If husband is not confident of being loyal, he will definitely hesitate in giving commitment which also make blunder in the bond.

Confidence got build up with continuous practice. If someone is having phobia with water or mathematics, practice is only solution to build confidence in ourselves. We need to deep dive repeatedly to overcome the phobia and excel with high confidence. If we were writing some examination and in middle of it, we are short of time, we may lose confidence and end up making the silly mistakes like addition of one-digit figures. We need to boost it up again by saying

Yes, I can. I have all required knowledge and skill to excel.

At some instance in life, it happens that you were on right track and doing great job for achieving the goal, but people who were having *"crabs in bucket mentality"* who tries to crush your moral and confidence. These people have such frame of mind like *"If I can't have it, neither can you"*. If you leave bunch of crabs in bucket, if any tries to move out of it, others pull it back resulting none of them able to escape out. The same phenomenon can be seen in our world of human as well. You need to check night and day if you were part of same occurrence by asking few questions to yourself

Whether have you experienced folks ask you to suppress your thoughts or ideas for which you were excited to showcase?

You were planning for starting new task or venture, but you were shown the negative impacts of it?

Not letting you to try or implement your new emerging idea?

If answer to these were coming to yes, it's time to move out that group. If you think leaving that group can impact your financial or personal life somehow, trust me being with them also doesn't yield any profit. You would be on losing side of yourself and end up with becoming the enemy for self-germination.

5

Courage and Passion

"Leadership is not about a title or a designation. It's about impact, influence, and inspiration.

Impact involves getting results, influence is about spreading the passion you

have for your work, and you have to inspire team-mates and customers."

By Robin S. Sharma

If human exist irrespective of race, religion, culture it's certain for having passion to follow, coinciding question is raised that how many ends up doing so. How many of us have that much courage to take risk for following what their inner soul desires but got suppressed with thoughts going through the mind considering the consequences of it. Passion doesn't need to match up with your parents or partner. It's not genetically aligned to anyone. You could find your inclination towards any activity which cherish your time and soul.

We have gone through a section about the confidence, which is dominant factor in one's life to lead. So, if you think you have the confidence to take up a chance to live your passion, you should have the courage to say yourself that YES, I will do it. YES, I can do it. That's all, hurdles will not be there anymore. Let your wings open making your soul fly. Everybody has wings to sail the world of their passion, only which restrain their steps is the courage inside them.

Though I don't consider for writing any set of questions related to passion as you must have answer but allow me to do so because I am also sailing through my passion journey.

We need to ponder on ourselves what your passion is?

What were the things you love the most to do?

Is there anything else which makes you happier out of your daily practice?

How much time you were taking out for doing it?

I need to be sure that you already had all these answers already with you in your mind, even before going through these set of questions. If not, no worries you don't need to be dishearten my dear, its never too late. Now you have the answers.

Some folks consider it to be a time-wasting activity saying out loud displaying themselves as sapient. It's observed that, people who follow their passion have efficient psychologically functioning, happier and successful compared to other section. We must have observed that during covid times a lot of human beings left their active job willingly to follow their passion, it's fascinating to observe that they were doing good in terms of peace of mind and fulfilling their financial needs at same time as becoming video-blogger showing their talent as actors, singers, stand-up comedian, food blogger, free lancers and list goes on.

Everyone must have heard "Do what makes you happy", "Follow your passion", although only few understood this or were seen doing what makes them happy. If you take out any name from the list triumphant like Bill Gates, Steve Jobs or Elon Musk you will realised that they were following their passion. Though the series of questions again arises

How can we do that?

From where we would get fundings?

We don't have time. How to manage it?

There could be a lot more questions as well. The only factor which can help anyone to do so and drives you to follow the journey of your passion is none other than COURAGE. There is a thin line between following your passion and ignoring your focus from it, it's the courage you need to break that ice. Courage now comes into the picture which can act as a fuel to boost you and lets you to give a thrust to cross the gravitational force of your thoughts and introducing the horizon of you passion where you can let yourself set free. You will find yourself in the abundance of stars which symbolise your achievements. You would be able to write your own story.

People must argue over time saying that they were short of it. My dear we are on earth, where days duration is twenty-four hours for everyone. I am not sure what makes you occupied that much intense that you were not able to take an hour in day or week for yourself. If your name is in Forbes list or some glamorous magazine cover page than I can't comment though. If not, then I would say stop fooling yourself saying so. Stop thinking with your mind for a second and listen to your soul who is begging to you desperately to live, fly, dance, stretching the wings of dreams and happiness with its own will without having any hesitation from your own mind.

6

Patience

"How poor were they that have no patience! What would did ever heal but by degrees?"

By William Shakespeare

Life is like a clock which goes on and it doesn't need any consent. Here comes the interesting part of it, you can redirect it the way you want to. You are the driver of your own life. You can choose the road to take, can travel to any destination you got on your mind. So, if anything comes on your way be it success or failure, it's you who has to handle it with your highly indispensable mind with great precision. Life will give you the taste of bitter failures and honeyed success as well. Always remember it depends on you how situations being handled in life for reaching your goal.

An adage

"Life gives you lemons, it's you who make the lemonade"

but what's next? No one talks about.

What to do with that lemonade?

Everyone is on their own journey to the ultimate destination. Some may feed themselves with the lemonade they have to cherish themselves. But there were few left who used that lemonade selling out to others wisely, making a lot of profits out of that, which they will use for themselves at the end. I will let you decide

Who is wise?

Among these in which category you find yourself?

The only difference among these group is of Patience. I must say the patience is one of the hardest quality one can have, but those who possess it would find themselves falling into the category of folks making profits with lemonade. Patience takes part in making vital decision makings, achieving the goals and hence gives out the profits to life making us less prone to any misstep. It can help us as guiding factor as traffic signals do.

Whenever the situation arises where you feels surrounded with all negativities, stressed out you need to take a deep breathe. You must be having a hold of your patience. I must warn you at this very moment that It won't be that's easy how its pretending to be. Holding patience is much harder than holding breathe under water for more than sixty seconds.

Patience is not only part of your work, speech, or actions rather I would say it's a lifestyle. It reflects a personality or even can change the human if someone start preaching of it.

"It's easier to find men who will volunteer to die,

than to find those who are willing to endure pain with patience"

By Julius Caesar

Till now hopes you got the idea of it. Now we have the questions

So according to you what is patience?

How much your lifestyle to aligned towards it?

Do you think you need to work on that part?

I am not sure about the answers you have for the first two questions, but if the answer to last question is NO then we need to ponder on it again. Humans have the tendency to lose patience, some give up on it easily while some have great grip.

Losing patience is like a storm, the more you lose blunder of large extent it would made. As I mentioned everyone has the tendency of losing it, but with practice you can increase the level of handling it. It's an art more you practice the more perfection you would attain. Learning an Art or Skill of patience one thing is required, and that is again patience.

Patience is the skill which needs to be inculcated in all socio-animal without having any exception of profession they belong to. Patience is that secret which enables any person to solve many rigid problems. It helps you to think and take actions rather rapidly start working towards the problem without giving a single thought about that.

No one can reap the fruit on very same day you sow the seed. The best example that usually comes to my mind while thinking about patience is Farming. One can have the joy and satisfaction of having a fruit from plant which nurtured by them patiently over long period of time. Every stage of it is critical and teaching great lessons out of it. Even parenting is another great example for patience which comes with a different virtue of life's responsibilities. Patience can change the environment at home if executed wisely. If parents patiently listen and learns about the problems or phase through which their children are going through, can help them to take a very good decisions in their children's favours. It can help the parents to make ready their children to face any challenge working as team and listening to each other.

If someone wants to get anything, be it a university degree, a good shape and healthy body, writing a book, preparation of food or even a good relationships patience plays critical role in the enhancement of it. One of the greatest speciality of this skill is that it helps you to solve the problems with a different angle or we can say it gives another eye to look at with major focus towards the resolution of it. You need to analyse yourself how patient you are by simple questions we have.

Were you able to find yourself in a situation where you jump directly for the resolution without doing any analysis?

Were you always eager to have results without putting efforts towards that?

If answers were either yes or no, don't need to worry about. In the era of automation and technology everyone wants the pace with their actions and better results without putting much hard work. The point which I want you ponder upon is doing analysis with patience before any action. Let suppose, If your sales were going down as a boss, you shouldn't be finding yourself in a situation where you were firing your sales and marketing department. The problem could lie in product itself and technical staff could be the culprit or even a better competitor is in marketplace which you were completely unaware of and sweeping your business out of the market.

It's acceptable that every human thinks to be perfectionist in his judgement taken. They consider themselves wise. Managements in many multinationals were also lacking this skill, which is more important to have. If someone thinks of having good business knowledge and communication makes them a great leader. The answer would be no. Patience is important to have as much critical business knowledge and other skills required. The leader with good patience would observe the criticality of business and her or his decisions would be really encouraging towards high profits of the organisation. She or He always tries to connect and enhancing the relationship with workers and colleagues to achieve a goal. We were in the era of innovation where thousands of start-ups were being opening every fiscal. For being an entrepreneur, one must be a person with great patience if she or he wants to build an empire. Its important because it gives the capability of not limiting yourself for learning new skills, building relationships, management of finances and not only creating a product but also innovating yourself by thinking out of the box.

Better patience level could help in being positive towards the problem, enhancing the resolution and creating happiness around us. It can help in limiting the anger and thus resulting the good health. The performance would be encouraging for sure with good decision-making capabilities.

7

Opportunity

"If somebody offers you an amazing opportunity but you are not sure you can do it,

say yes

then learn how to do it later."

By Richard Branson

For us the opportunity means a chance for changing the circumstances in positive outlook for our growth, learn to do better. We need to be proactive towards it to identify.

Opportunity doesn't come with some musical band and make announcements for you to be grabbed.

If I would say no one is deprived of opportunities around them, many would start a fatal debate. If they would be asked what does an entrepreneur mean to them? For me Entrepreneur were among those who seek a gap in between the problem and need for the society. To fill that gap, she or he is the one who creates opportunities for themselves.

First and foremost, thing you need to do is throughout self-examine, and you should be able to answer few questions to yourself

What you want to achieve?

What is your current situation?

How can you reach to your goal?

What potential opportunity you see now?

What were expectations with opportunity you consider should have?

Once you have the answers to these questions you will be able to decide and build the path for yourself. It could be possible that you got stuck in some question and won't be able to proceed to the next. It's completely fine. It's a real time opportunity where you must dive into your thoughts to find out the answers for your real Opportunity.

Sometimes it could lead to a situation where you need to decide to make some sacrifices to grab it. You won't need to regret on such sacrifices because if you have made decision in choosing your path you should move on with courage without thinking of taking U-Turn as you need to keep in mind that you have paid the cost for it. Sacrifices could be related to any promised incentive or promotion by your management, or it could be anything that can limit your action of moving out from your refuge. Remember no one will come and feed into your mouth, it's you who has to take steps for anything you want into your plate of success. If you want to click a snap of sunrise tomorrow, you need to set an alarm, you need to wake up before the sunrise, and foremost you need to sacrifice your deary sleep to grab that opportunity. Let suppose if you have missed it with any reason or excuse, you can do it next day as well, but what if it was some astronomic phenomenon happened for which you missed the snap. So, you need to understand the criticality of situation and clarity about sacrifices.

Opportunities for sure won't come with excuses. No matter how many resources you would have, and situation aligned to it. If you were the person with excuses, you would be missing out the great opportunities. Opportunity is like a clock, once missed it won't be back no matter how hard you try. If you were able to get it, it won't taste the same how it had earlier. Everybody were born with their special skill hidden internally which we were totally unaware of it. Sometimes we were able to discover the talent in form of hobby. We need to turn up the coin on which our special powers engraved. The importance of that findings is to turn our very owned powers in creating the opportunities for our selves.

What you think about your special power?

Have you already discovered it?

Were you able to channelize it properly?

Once you start self-exploration going through the analytics of the question appropriately, you would be surprised to find more potential opportunistic answers in your bucket. All you have to do is traverse though your mind with broad approach. Many new elements you would be discovered. Please don't hesitate if your mind with getting flooded with more questions. It's a great symbol that you were really diving deeply into the space of your mind to find out the answers of your unsolved mysteries.

"If Opportunity doesn't knock, build a door"

By Milton Berle

Every closed door comes with a problem to get solved with your efforts, patience, and courage behind which opportunities lies. It's you, who need to explore around yourself with self help to find the right set of keys for unlocking the door. Never hesitate or discourage yourself seeing the problems, because no one knows you become an exception in finding the answers in search of opportunities. Every great theory exists was a problem before it was discovered.

Remember if you were doing this exploration, don't stuck with finding answers. You were doing it for your enhancement only. You need to act upon these so that you move towards the opportunity, and hence your goal with help of it. You should encourage your internal self and be focused on your opportunities until goals were achieved.

8
Belief

"The moment you doubt whether you can fly, you cease forever to be able to do it."
– By James Matthew Barrie

We were living in twenty first century with thrashed mentality of focusing on others what they were doing rather concentrating on ourselves. I also believe that no one wants intervention to their own life, but world is really interested in others. There is nothing wrong or right with this approach, but we end up with crashing a lot of time and a thought of comparison arises as well. If you were taking it in a positive outlook then we are on the correct path, but if you were suppressing your self-confidence and beliefs, believe me we would be going to make a blunder with our life.

Each species on earth exists with different traits, and same applies to humans as well. Each human being is having their own skills and characteristics. With these traits and the environment in which we were growing imparts some beliefs and thoughts inside us. These beliefs are the directing factor of our life, it could lead you to lavish life or could result in destruction as well. The beliefs can direct your actions required for any situation that revolves around you. Some of the questions you need to ponder like

What makes your anger to its peak?

How you suppress or express your thoughts?

How you chose the circle around yourself?

What makes you irritates most and your action towards it?

These were just some of the examples on which you need to make clear understanding for yourself. Once you figure it out the root cause and solution, make sure next time you should be able to implement those for betterment. You must agree with me that many of our thoughts were environment dependent. Let suppose your child or younger sibling is doing some blunder but you consider it to be a childish act which made you laugh, on other instant same act could make you feel ridiculous if performed in front of your friends by same child.

If you are having negotiation with client for some major deal, it's inevitable that off topic talks can't happen. It could lead to a situation where your thoughts were not matching up with client, and you might need to pretend agreed just to win that deal, what if you weren't. So, we can conclude that beliefs can make you win or lose a deal, even if you were great salesman.

There is no hard and fast rule to handle situations where you see the thoughts were not on same page with other person. You should be targeting to make a profit of any situation you encounter with belief on yourself without limiting or hesitating. Belief is what that can help you boosting the confidence of doing tasks and resulting in positive manner.

No one can control the thoughts and beliefs of others but can handle their own like a pro. It's time to introspect your unique thoughts and beliefs for yourself. The combination of your thoughts about yourself can mirror you the personality you are. We shouldn't comment on anyone's belief or tries to make any alteration because you will end up with ruining the relation.

If anyone wants to grow in their life they can't unless they have the essence of self-realisation and belief of doing it. Self-belief is the principle of life that needs to be implemented so we can look forward to grow with putting less efforts compared to the task for which your were assigned to accomplish by some external factors. Not having belief on self can create a situation where you want to grow but feel the high resistance, which you were totally unaware of it. Self-belief is driving factor for all other personality traits which were necessarily required in growth for any. Let us look at some questions

Do you feel demotivated for any task you pick?

Are you losing interest in doing anything?

Do you find a situation where you see yourself having low amount of energy?

If answers to these questions were somewhere yes, then we really need to wake up. It's high time to look around yourself and believe in yourself. The very first person who can believe in you is none other than yourself. If you would lose self-belief, trust me no one would have trust on you resulting of which closing the doors of opportunity.

"If you are insecure, guess what? The rest of the world is too.

Do not overestimate the competition and underestimate yourself.

You are better than you think."

By T. Harv Eker

If you have self-belief that you can do or achieve your goal, this statement implies that you would surely be getting the success, no matters how many undesirable situations would be there. You would be able to tackle all like a monster truck on road with mini. It can give you another aspect to look towards the problem. Believing on self can gives you the clear image to proceed and opening the self-help book for you.